# has Fun

BBC CHiLDReN'S BOOKS

## PINGU AND PINGA AT HOME

Pingu's mum and dad were going out for the evening to a concert.

Pingu and Pinga watched as Mum put on her new hat. How pretty she looked.

Mum and Dad waved goodbye. "Be good,"
said Dad.

Pinga started to cry.

"Don't worry. We won't be long," said Mum.

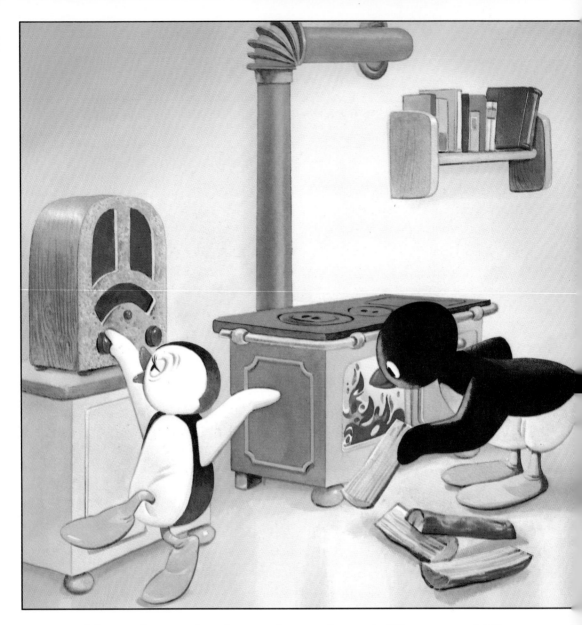

The minute the front door closed, Pingu and Pinga
leaped out of bed.

"I want to dance," said Pinga and turned the
radio on loud.

"I'm hungry," said Pingu and stoked up the fire.

Pinga screamed with delight as Pingu tossed a pancake in the air. Higher and higher it went until – oops – it stuck to the ceiling!

Pingu's mum was enjoying the music at the
concert, but Pingu's dad kept nodding off to sleep.
"Wake up," hissed Mum. "Everyone can hear
you snoring."

Back at home Pingu and Pinga were having fun.
Pingu was busy emptying the big cupboard.

"Just look at me," said Pinga, trying on Mum's
wedding hat.

Soon there was chaos everywhere.
"Beep, beep! Here we go!" yelled Pingu as he
pushed Pinga round the·room in a hat-box.

    At the concert Mum was beginning to miss Pingu and Pinga.

    "Do you think they're all right on their own?" she asked Dad anxiously as she wiped a tear from her eye.

Pingu and Pinga were at that very moment splashing about in a bath full of bubbles. They were pretending to be seals.

   Suddenly Pingu noticed the time. Mum and Dad
would be back soon. He and Pinga had to work
very hard putting everything back where it
belonged.

But no matter how hard he pushed, Pingu couldn't
shut the cupboard doors. He wondered how
everything had ever fitted in.

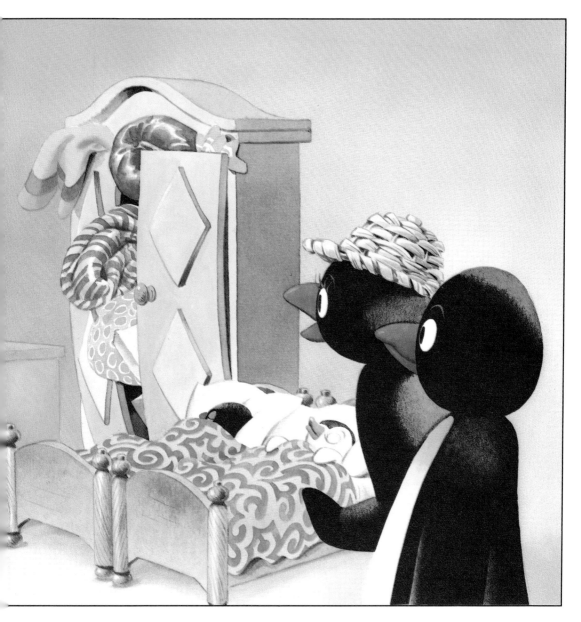

When Pingu's mum and dad got home they found
two little sleeping beauties.

But then Mum noticed the heaving cupboard.
"*What* has been going on?" she cried.

"We couldn't get to sleep on our own," explained
Pingu. "We missed you too much."

"That's all right," said Pingu's mum. "We missed
you, too!" And Dad gave Pinga a nice, warm hug.

## SCHOOL TIME

On his way to school one morning Pingu met his friend Robby the seal.

"I'll come to school with you," said Robby and together the two friends zoomed down an icy slope.

Robby wanted to wear Pingu's satchel and to
have a look round the school. Pingu showed him
his desk and the blackboard.

At that moment the teacher rang the bell for class
to begin. Robby quickly dived into a nearby hole in
the ice before anyone could see him.

Today they were going to learn about underwater
life. Ping had to dive into the water and tell the
others what he could see.

Ping came back and drew the fish he had seen on the blackboard.

"Phew," thought Pingu. "He didn't spot Robby."

Pingo dived into the water next.

"The only fish down there is the one that's been eaten," he said and drew it in the blackboard.

Pingu started to laugh.

"I think there's a seal in the water and he ate the
fish," said Pingu, drawing a picture of Robby on the
blackboard.

The others all shook their heads.

Pingu went over to the water and held a fish over the hole. Sure enough Robby leaped up and took a bite out of it.

"You see, I was right," said Pingu.

"This is my friend Robby," said Pingu. "He wanted to see my school."

"We might as well put him to work, then," said the teacher.

Robby was sent down into the water. First of all he came back with a very big fish. The teacher pinned it on the blackboard.

Before long Robby had collected all sorts of different creatures. The penguins enjoyed tossing them around.

But now they had to get down to some work.
Ping didn't know the name of the big flat fish.
Pingu was longing to tell him.

Pingu felt very silly when he couldn't remember
the last creature's name. But Robby helped him by
writing it quickly on the blackboard.

"Good old Robby," thought Pingu. "If only he
could come to school with me every day."

## GRANDPA IS ILL

The telephone was ringing in Pingu's house. Before Mum could reach it, Pinga had answered it.

"Is that you, Grandpa?" she said. "Your voice sounds funny."

Grandpa was ill. Mum was going straight round
to see him.

"You must behave yourself if you come with me,"
she said to Pingu who was fooling about.

Poor Grandpa didn't look at all well.

"Don't come too close," he said.

"Just say hello from where you are," said Mum anxiously.

Pingu was sad to see Grandpa looking miserable.
He wanted to cheer him up and so he found a way
of shaking Grandpa's hand without touching him.

While Mum made Grandpa some soup, Pingu
and Pinga began to explore Grandpa's cupboard.
They were soon making a lot of noise.

"Oh, my poor head!" moaned Grandpa.

"Go outside at once," ordered Mum. "And just play
quietly on your own. I haven't time to look after you
as well."

Pingu and Pinga see-sawed together outside. But the higher they went, the louder Pinga screamed. Mum stormed outside and scolded them again.

They played football next. But Pinga wasn't very
good in goal and all the snowballs Pingu kicked at
her thudded hard against the igloo door.

Suddenly the door opened and – SPLAT – Mum
got hit in the face with a snowball! Pinga laughed
and laughed.

"Go straight home," said Mum furiously, "and
wait there until I've finished looking after Grandpa."
Pinga had never seen Mum look so angry.

Back at home Pingu drew spots all over himself
and Pinga.

"Mum will have to come back and look after us
now," he said.

Mum was just rubbing some ointment on
Grandpa's head when the telephone rang. It was
Pingu to say that he and Pinga had a nasty rash.

Mum was shocked to see Pingu and Pinga, but
she soon realised that they were only teasing.
"What a relief," she said and they all began to
laugh.

Published by BBC Books, a division of BBC Enterprises Limited, Woodlands, 80 Wood Lane, London W12 0TT
First published in Hardback 1991. Illustrations by Tony Wolf. Original text by Sibylle von Flüe.
This edition © BBC Books by arrangement with Dami Editore 1993. Reprinted 1993 three times. Reprinted 1994.
PINGU © Editoy A G Bertschikon 1991. ISBN 0 563 40308 X
Printed and bound in Great Britain by Cambus Litho, East Kilbride